Tallulah's Tutu

First Position

Second Position

Third Position

Fourth Position   Fifth Position

Tallulah's Tutu

by MARILYN SINGER

Illustrations by
ALEXANDRA BOIGER

Houghton Mifflin Harcourt | Boston | New York

Thanks to Steve Aronson, Jennifer Greene and the other
good folks at Clarion Books, Laurie Shayler, and, especially,
Cara Gargano, ballet teacher extraordinaire. —M.S.

The text was set in Pastonchi MT Std.
The illustrations were executed in watercolor, as well as watercolor mixed with gouache
and egg yolk, on Fabriano watercolor paper.

www.hmhco.com

The Library of Congress has catalogued the hardcover edition as follows:
Singer, Marilyn.
Tallulah's tutu/by Marilyn Singer; illustrated by Alexandra Boiger
p. cm.
Summary: Tallulah takes ballet lessons and eagerly awaits her coveted tutu, which,
she learns, she must work hard to earn.
[1. Ballet dancing—Fiction. 2. Tutus (Ballet skirts)—Fiction.]
I. Boiger, Alexandra, ill. II. Title.
PZ7.S6172Tal 2011
[E]—dc22
2010005441

ISBN: 978-0-547-17353-5 hardcover
ISBN: 978-0-544-66835-5 paperback

Manufactured in China
SCP 10 9 8 7 6 5 4

4500732105

To the ballet students at the Third Street Music School Settlement
—M.S.

To Xenia and Sal, with love
—A.B.

TALLULAH just knew she could be a great ballerina—
if only she had a tutu.

"And maybe a lesson or two," her mother said with a wink.

So the next day, Tallulah went to her very first ballet class.
The kids wore leotards and pink tights. All except one.

He had on black pants. **A boy in ballet? Well, HE won't get a tutu.** Tallulah giggled.

"Are you with us, Tallulah?" asked her teacher.

Tallulah decided she'd better pay attention.
She watched closely.

She turned out her feet and curved her
hands near her hips in first position.

She bent her knees in a plié.
She did it perfectly.

I am an excellent ballerina, she thought.
And soon, I'll get a tutu.

At the end of class, the teacher
told them what a good job they'd done.
Tallulah waited for her tutu.

But instead she got a hug.
"Good job," her teacher said.

Tallulah decided that her tutu must be coming from Paris. They would fly it in next week.

Tallulah practiced every day. "Look at my beautiful arms," she said on the way to class. "Look at my perfect finish!"

She grinned a big grin as she stood at the barre. "What color tutu do you want?" she asked the girl in front of her. "I want lavender!" She pointed to some September asters blooming outside the window.

"Tallulah, look in the mirror. Can you make your back straighter?" her teacher said.

Tallulah could. She jumped her heels apart to second position. She pointed her toe in a tendu. She circled her foot on the floor in a rond de jambe.

I am a fabulous ballerina, Tallulah told herself. I'm going to get my tutu right after class.

But this time all she got was a kiss on the top of her head.
"Keep it up, Tallulah. You're doing well," said her teacher.

Tallulah figured the delivery truck broke down. Her
tutu must be stuck in New Jersey. They would drive
it in next week.

At home, Tallulah showed her mother everything she'd learned.
Her little brother, Beckett, watched. Then she practiced some more.

At her third lesson, she could hardly keep still. "One-two-three. One-two-three," she sang to the boy next to her. "A tunic for you, a tutu for me." She whirled around and bumped his leg.

"Tallulah, stay in your own space, please," her teacher said.

"Whoops," Tallulah said.

She shifted one foot in front of the other in third position.

She put one foot against her other knee in a passé.

She did a relevé by standing on her toes.

I'm
the best
ballerina
in the world,
Tallulah said
to herself.
Today I'll get
my tutu for sure!

But there was no tutu for Tallulah. No tutu at all.

"Where is it?" she asked her teacher.

"Where is what?"

"My tutu."

Tallulah's teacher leaned down and put her arm around her. "You have to wait awhile, Tallulah. It takes time and a lot of practice to earn your tutu."

Tallulah stamped her foot. It did not feel good to do that in a ballet slipper. "That's not fair!" she cried. "A ballerina needs a tutu, and she needs it now!"

Tallulah decided she wasn't going to practice any more ballet.
She told her mother that she wasn't going to show her any more steps.
And she wasn't going to go to class ever again.

"Really?" said her mother. "But I thought you loved ballet."

"*I* love ballet," said Beckett, even though he'd never taken a class.

"Well, *I don't.* I'm not even going to *think* about ballet anymore,"
Talullah declared.

But everything kept reminding Tallulah of ballet. Her neighbor's basset hound always stood in second position. The kitchen clock constantly performed ronds de jambe. The serving spoon at dinner was forever doing tendus.

And everywhere she went, Tallulah couldn't help *dancing* ballet.

She always did a plié when she patted the neighbor's dog,

and she couldn't go by a store window without doing a beautiful finish

or pass a park bench without using it as a barre.

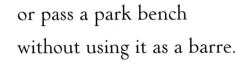

Then, one day in the supermarket,
she heard tinkly music over the loudspeakers.
It was the same music the pianist played
in her class. Tallulah couldn't stop herself.

Passés,
relevés,
tendus . . . she did them all!

She pirouetted around the store.

When she finished, the shoppers applauded. Except for one girl.
She was wearing a lavender tutu. "I want to dance like that," she said.
"I've already got the tutu."

"Maybe you need a lesson or two. Or *twenty*-two," Tallulah said.

"And lots of practice as well." She looked at her mother and winked.

The next day she went back to class. "I'm glad to see you, Tallulah," said her teacher.

Tallulah beamed. "I'm glad to see you, too," she said. Then she took her place at the barre.

I am a very, very good dancer, she thought.
And **I WILL** get my tutu . . . someday.

And she did. Except it wasn't lavender.
It was as red as the roses blooming that June.

First Position

Second Position

Third Position

Fourth Position   Fifth Position